Would You You Believe It?

Edited by Kate Agnew

Illustrated by Garry Parsons

EGMONT

First published in Great Britain in 2003
by Egmont Books Ltd
239 Kensington High Street, London W8 6SA

ISBN 1 4052 0520 2

10 9 8 7 6 5 4 3 2 1

A CIP catalogue record for this title is available from the British Library

Typeset by Dorchester Typesetting Group Ltd
Printed and bound in Great Britain by Mackays of Chatham Ltd, Chatham, Kent

Contents

Introduction

Magical and mysterious stories have long
been a favourite with readers of all ages.
For some, it's the stories' other worldliness
that makes them special, for others it's that
intriguing glimpse of a world in which the
everyday is made strange and the curious
familiar. Perhaps you like stories about
trainee wizards and witches, or tales of epic
battles and the powerful struggle between
good and evil, or maybe it's the quiet
magic that some days seems to be

Would You Believe It?

everywhere around us, that touches your imagination . . .

In Ann Jungman's *Jackie and the Baked Bean Stalk* we see the day-to-day world dramatically turned upside down by the discovery of a giant at the top of the newly-sprouted baked bean stalk. A fresh and witty take on the story of *Jack and the Beanstalk,* this amusing tale will have you chuckling out loud. Elinor Hodgson's magic, on the other hand, is quietly lyrical, a dreamy tale to capture the imagination. Then there's the macabre creepiness of the *Unlucky Charm* that Ben's grandfather gives him or the sinister tap-tap-tapping of the hooves of a ghost horse in *Cross Your Heart.* If you enjoy being scared these are definitely stories for you.

In Pippa Goodhart's enchanting *Someone Elsie,* magic creeps silently into Rose and Daisy's night-time world – a subtle,

Introduction

beautiful kind of magic that is as eerie as it is lovely. The magic in Rachel Anderson's Light than Bright is of a very different sort – a humorous, quirky magic that sits wittily alongside ordinary life. Perhaps as you read this anthology you'll begin to think that you too live in a magical world, or perhaps the haunting scariness lurking beneath some of these stories will make you thankful that your place is in the real world. Whether you like the chilling or the dreamy, the familiar or the weird, there is sure to be something here for you.

Kate Agnew

Lighter Than Bright

—

RACHEL ANDERSON

Last year, in the town where I live, it got very dark. And stayed dark.

'Well, that's winter for you!' said my mum. 'Short days. Long nights. You'll get used to it by the time you're my age.'

I said, 'But I don't *want* to get used to it. And nor does Lizzie.' She's my little sister. Sometimes, for her sake, I pretended not to mind the dark. I was trying to set a good example.

Would You Believe It?

Roundabout Christmas-time, things got a bit better, specially when we had our tree up with the sparkly decorations, and the red candles on the windowsill which Mum let me light with the matches, so long as I kept them away from Lizzie. And all down the High Street, too, there were fancy coloured decorations.

'Look, Lizzie!' said Mum, pointing up. 'Watch the pretty fairy lights!'

The lights were flashing on and off, and on again, all down the street.

I told Mum, 'It's just an electrical circuit.'

But my mum is the type of person who likes to believe in fairies, and making wishes when you see two magpies together, and throwing salt over your shoulder to ward off bad omens, and all that kind of stuff.

I said, 'I don't think you should tell babies facts which aren't true.'

Lighter Than Bright

Mum said, 'You're right, Matty. Though sometimes the difficulty is sorting what's absolute truth from what's an imaginative truth.'

I didn't understand what she meant, apart from the first bit about me being right. I liked that bit.

Once Christmas was over, and the decorations were taken down, we were back in with the gloomy dark nights. I had to check under Lizzie's cot for ghosties even though I know they aren't real.

Mum said, 'It'll be all right, so long as the earth keeps on turning. The days are definitely getting longer. We'll soon be at the Equinox.'

That's always an important day in Mum's magical calendar. It's when day and night are of exactly equal length and she has to throw raw eggs over the rooftop to bring good fortune in the coming quarter.

Would You Believe It?

In my opinion, it's a waste of good eggs. It's also messy, which makes playing football in the back garden slippery.

Now, what happened on the day of the Equinox was probably nothing to do with eggs, but it was most peculiar and almost strange enough to make me believe in Mum's magic.

First, there was sunshine. All day.

'Look at that, Lizzie!' I said to my baby sister. 'That's called the sun!' It had been so long since we'd seen it, I thought she might not know what it was. Lizzie gurgled and clapped her hands.

'Mum,' I said. 'Can I take Lizzie out in the buggy? Just down to the green and back?'

'Very well. But be careful, won't you?'

'Of course.'

I thought some of my mates might be down at the green. But it was deserted

apart from some seagulls at the pond. So I kicked my football about on my own while Lizzie sat in her buggy and watched. I was looking forward to when she'd be old enough to join in because it can be a bit boring playing by yourself.

'OK, Lizzie,' I said, picking up my football. 'Time for home.'

As I pushed the buggy across the green, I looked carefully at the sky to see if I could notice the turning of the earth.

I explained to Lizzie, 'You see, it's turning all the time. That's what makes the night and the day and the changing of the seasons.' Even if she's too young to understand, I think it's important for her to start hearing some sound scientific facts as well as Mum's magic.

She waved her hand and giggled.

We both gazed up at the big blue springtime sky. Suddenly, one of the

Would You Believe It?

dazzling sunbeams bounced off the ripples on the surface of the pond and shot into my eyes. It was so bright that for a moment I couldn't see anything.

I blinked hard. I half-expected to discover I'd lost my sight. Worse than that – I'd lost my visibility. I could see the football there in front of me but I couldn't see my hands holding it. Nor the rest of me.

Nor Lizzie. The buggy was empty. Or seemed to be.

'Lizzie! Where are you?'

She chuckled merrily and the buggy shook. I bent down and felt around. She was still safely strapped in. Unfortunately, she'd gone invisible too.

I ran home faster than I've ever run before.

I hammered on the front door. Mum took ages to hear. She was out the back

clearing up thrown eggs.

I shouted through the letter box. 'Mum, Lizzie's gone invisible!'

At last she came to let us in. When she realised what had happened, she was very annoyed with me.

'Oh, Matty! How *could* you? I thought you were to be trusted. You've done this on purpose, haven't you? Just to vex me because you knew I was going to be busy with the egg-throwing!'

I said I was sorry. She just went on grumbling.

'I *warned* you to be careful.'

'I *was*. I thought you meant about not stepping on the lines in the pavement in case the bears came up and got us.'

She sighed. 'Oh, Matty! Can't you tell the difference between real magic and pretend? That's just a game, like ghosties under the beds. I meant, be careful about

the power of the sun.'

Lizzie began grizzling. She was hungry for her tea. But it was difficult for Mum spooning mashed banana into Lizzie's open mouth when she couldn't see where it was.

I tried to help by making funny faces to make Lizzie laugh. It usually worked. But not that day.

That evening, Mum did all the tricks she knew. Burning feathers. Spitting at the moon. Burying a dried toad she happened to find. Mixing up pink syrups. Singing nursery rhymes backwards. In the end, she gave up and started to get Lizzie ready for bed.

I said, 'You'd better not give her a bath. It wouldn't be safe. Suppose she slipped over in the water?'

Mum said, 'All right. She can make do with a lick and promise.'

That meant a quick wipe with a

Lighter Than Bright

damp flannel.

I went up to bed a bit later on. I had to whistle for Mum to come and give me a goodnight kiss, so she'd know where my cheek was.

Mum said, 'I'm sorry I was so cross with you earlier on. I know you wouldn't deliberately let anything bad happen to Lizzie. Maybe it'll be all right tomorrow.'

But next morning, Lizzie and I were still completely invisible.

'There's nothing for it,' Mum said, disappointed. 'I shall have to consult Dr Grundy.'

I hated having to go to the surgery.

I said, 'That waiting room's always full of sickly people. We're sure to catch something bad.'

Mum said, 'It couldn't be worse than what you've got already.'

I decided to keep quiet. But that only

upset Mum even more because she said if I wasn't talking, she didn't know where I was.

Dr Grundy is a glum old man. He said, very mournfully, 'It's definitely a mild case of invisibility they've got.'

Mum snapped back, 'Any fool can see that. But what's to be done about it?'

So Dr Grundy asked me, 'What day of the week were you born on?' I was born on a Monday, which used to be a sign of woe. However, all these superstitions keep changing. And new ones keep arriving from the East.

Then he examined me and Lizzie as well as he could and said to Mum, 'You'll be glad to know it's definitely not contagious. So they can mix with other children if you wish. Not that I advise it. Children these days! Pwah! Like the new superstitions. Nothing like as good as the old ones.'

Lighter Than Bright

Mum said, 'But will they recover?'

'Alas,' said Dr Grundy woefully, 'the medical world still doesn't fully understand the causes of total invisibility. None of my learned colleagues has discovered the quick cure. It may go of its own accord. Or the children may have to wait until the time of the Vernal Equinox for a reversal of their fortunes.'

'Not till the *next* Equinox!' gasped Mum. She was obviously a bit upset.

I said, 'When's that?'

'The autumn,' said Mum, almost crying. 'Six months away.'

Dr Grundy glanced over at his wall-calendar. 'Vernal Equinox: 22 September. By the way,' he turned to Mum, 'you weren't doing any of that over-the-rooftop-raw-egg-throwing yesterday, were you? That sometimes sets it off – the collision of science and superstition.'

Would You Believe It?

Mum looked uneasy. 'Thank you for your diagnosis, Dr Grundy,' she said, groped around for Lizzie on the floor, gathered her up and made briskly for the door. 'Come along now, Matty,' she said. We went home.

Soon, it was the Easter holidays. Lizzie and I played out on the green most days, though there was never anyone else there who'd play with us. But Mum said, 'At least you're getting plenty of fresh air and that'll do you good.'

We didn't have to wait till autumn, thank goodness. We faded back to visibility gradually. It seemed to be quite random. The first part of Lizzie to reappear was the top of her curly head. Next her nose. Then her big smile.

For me, it was my right foot which came back before anything else. This was good.

Lighter Than Bright

Because it made playing football much easier.

By the start of the new term, we were both entirely back to normal again. Soon, I'd forgotten all about it. Until, that is, I grew a big pink wart on my thumb.

I showed it to Mum. She said, 'I know the very cure for a wart like that. We must rinse your hands in an empty silver basin, at midnight, by the light of the full moon.'

I said, 'Thanks, Mum, but no thanks. I'd rather have Dr Grundy's opinion.'

So Mum made an appointment for me at the surgery.

Dr Grundy said, 'If you bind your hand in bayleaves, then bury them beneath a molehill, all your warts will vanish in a trice.'

I said, 'I've only got one wart.'

But Dr Grundy is an old man. And he wasn't listening. 'Next patient, please,' he

Would You Believe It?

said mournfully.

I went home. I told Mum, 'I've had enough of magic.'

She gave me a hug and said, 'You may be right, Matty. Sometimes, if you do nothing at all, the result is precisely the same.'

So that's what I did. And, sure enough, after a few months of doing nothing about it, the wart on my thumb, just like the invisibility, went away entirely of its own accord.

Jackie and the
Baked Bean Stalk

—

ANN JUNGMAN

Oh no! thought Jackie and her heart sank.
Not baked beans again!

Ever since the big steel works in the
town had been closed, Jackie's dad had
been out of work. That meant they had
baked beans every other day.

'Come on, eat up,' said her mum.

'But I hate them, Mum.'

'Baked beans are cheap and full of
nutrition.'

Would You Believe It?

Secretly, Jackie threw the baked beans out of the kitchen window.

The next morning, Jackie woke up and noticed that something green was blocking most of the light.

Whatever can it be? she thought and she got dressed and ran out into the garden. There was a huge beanstalk that reached right up to the clouds.

'Just like *Jack and the Beanstalk*,' cried Jackie. 'It must be from my baked beans. I wonder where it goes.'

And she began to climb, up into the clouds.

When she finally got to the top, Jackie stopped to look around. As far as she could see there were rolling hills covered in spring flowers and birds singing in the trees.

What a lovely place, thought Jackie. I've never been anywhere this beautiful, not even Blackpool.

16 ☆

Then, in the distance, she saw a castle.

'That must be the castle of the giant Jack killed,' she said to herself.

So, feeling safe, Jackie walked on. Once at the castle, she saw a beautiful garden, with flowers as big as trees.

'It's all so neat and tidy,' muttered Jackie. 'Someone must be taking care of it.'

The huge wooden door was open, so Jackie plucked up her courage and went in.

'Well!' came a loud booming voice. 'What have we here?'

Jackie looked up and there, towering over her, stood the giant.

'Please, sir,' cried Jackie, trying hard not to sound scared, 'my name is Jackie and I climbed up the baked bean stalk.'

'It's that pesky boy Jack again,' the giant shouted to his wife.

The giant's wife came running in and knelt down to look at Jackie.

17

'Not him again. I'll deal with him, just leave him to me.'

Then she looked down at Jackie and a big smile spread over her face.

'Why, that's not Jack, that's a little girl.'

'A girl!' shouted the giant. 'What's she doing here? I've never seen a girl before,' and he picked Jackie up in his huge hand and put her on the table in front of him.

'Good morning, sir,' said Jackie politely. Then she raised her voice so that he could hear her. 'Pleased to meet you.'

'Well, if that doesn't beat everything,' said the giant's wife, and she sat down next to her husband and stared at Jackie.

'After all these centuries, to be visited by a little girl – and she's wearing trousers. Whatever is the world coming to?'

'Most girls wear trousers nowadays,' Jackie told them. 'I'm not unusual.'

'I hope you're not related to that nasty

boy Jack,' said the giant's wife. 'We had no end of problems with him. No manners at all.'

'Oh no,' Jackie assured her. 'I know my name is Jackie, but it's short for Jacqueline.'

'Now that is a pretty name,' said the giant. 'We'll call you Jacqueline, won't we Mother?'

'Oh yes,' agreed his wife. 'Now, my dear, tell us what brings you here.'

So Jackie told them all about the steel works in Trumplington closing down and about her father being out of work and having no money and having to eat baked beans three times a week. The giant and his wife were very sympathetic and got out the biscuit tin.

'I made them myself,' said the giant's wife holding out a huge biscuit. Jackie broke off a tiny bit and ate it.

'It's very nice,' she said. 'You are a

good cook.'

The giant and his wife beamed.

'I hope I'm not keeping you from your work,' said Jackie.

'Oh no!' roared the giant. 'I retired years ago.'

'So you don't eat people any more?' asked Jackie nervously.

'Good heavens, no,' said the giant and he laughed. 'Haven't done that in a long while, no teeth see,' and he opened his mouth wide and bent down so Jackie got a good view. Jackie stood on tiptoe to look inside.

'Oh dear, I hope that doesn't mean that you're hungry all the time.'

'Well, no,' said the giant, 'but it's hard to find anything soft that's tasty to eat.'

'Baked beans,' yelled Jackie. 'Let's go and pick some from my baked bean stalk.'

So the three of them set off across the

fields with a huge basket and soon it was filled with beans.

When they got back, the giant's wife boiled the beans in a huge cauldron. When they were soft she put some on a plate for the giant and kept some for herself. They munched away but looked rather miserable.

'They're very good for you,' Jackie told them.

'That's as may be,' grumbled the giant, 'but they're boring, very boring.'

'What you need to pep them up is tomato sauce,' declared Jackie.

'We've got plenty of tomatoes in the garden,' said the giant's wife.

So Jackie climbed into the basket and went out into the garden with the giant's wife.

'You can call me Mrs Giant, Jacqueline dear,' said the giant's wife.

21

Would You Believe It?

'And shall I call the giant, Mr Giant?' asked Jackie.

'Oh yes, I think he'd like that,' said Mrs Giant, as she placed four huge tomatoes gently in the basket next to Jackie. It seemed like a good moment to ask Mrs Giant how it was the giant was still alive, so Jackie cleared her throat and said, 'I hope you don't mind me asking, but down on the earth we all think that Jack killed the giant when the giant tried to climb down the beanstalk.'

Mrs Giant put down her basket and laughed.

'Oh, is that what the horrid boy put about? What a giggle. No, all Jack did was play dirty tricks and steal things. We were so keen to see the end of him, my husband pretended he was going to climb down the beanstalk. Jack got so scared he cut the beanstalk down. We were delighted; he fell

right into our trap. After that we had a bit of peace.'

'So Jack didn't kill a giant?'

'No! I mean, Jackie, we're not daft, we know a beanstalk couldn't bear our weight. Just wait till I tell Mr Giant, he'll have a good laugh.'

'Now some onions,' said Jackie as they passed a vast onion patch.

On the way back to the house, Jackie saw some enormous basil plants and grabbed some. Back in the kitchen, Mrs Giant got out a huge frying pan and fried the onions and then the tomatoes.

'Add a bit of salt and pepper and some basil,' suggested Jackie.

'Oh, she's wonderful, isn't she, Mother?' said the giant, sniffing happily. 'Oh I do like girls.'

Mrs Giant nodded as she spooned the tomato sauce all over the beans.

Would You Believe It?

They both took a spoonful of the
new mix.

'Wonderful!' cried the giant. 'I love it, I
love these baked beans.'

'Delicious,' agreed Mrs Giant, 'we can
eat this every day.'

But while Jackie and the two giants were
having a good time, her parents noticed
her absence.

'My little girl,' wept Jackie's mother.

'Maybe she's gone up there,' said her dad
and he went out and shook the beanstalk.

'Jackie, are you up there? Come on
down if you are, your mum's getting
very upset.'

But Jackie was far away talking to the
giants and didn't hear him.

'I'm going up after her,' said Jackie's dad.

'No, no,' wept her mum. 'You may not be
able to help her. She might have met up

with the giant. That brute would have eaten Jack in one gulp if he hadn't been too smart for him. Get the police – don't go up there alone?'

A few minutes later, the police came to the house and looked up at the beanstalk in amazement.

'How did it get there in the first place?' asked the policeman.

'Our Jackie doesn't like baked beans,' said her father. 'We think she may have thrown them out of the window.'

'Oh,' nodded the policeman, 'a bit like *Jack and the Beanstalk*. Well, if she's up there she may have met a giant.'

At this, Jackie's mother shrieked. 'That's what we're worried about. Oh, my poor Jackie.'

'Don't you worry yourself, Madam,' said the policeman. 'We know how to deal with giants.'

25

Would You Believe It?

And he rang the station.

'Send round twenty men and an ambulance and a fire engine – we've got a beanstalk to climb.'

A minute later, there was a deafening sound of sirens as the fire engine, the ambulance and four police cars all came screaming round the corner and into the street.

Jackie's dad and the police sergeant went up the beanstalk first, followed by ten policemen with strong pulleys dragging the ambulance, followed by the doctor and the nurses, with ten more policemen and the firemen pulling up the fire engine.

Mr and Mrs Giant were just finishing their fifth plate of baked beans and tomato sauce when suddenly they heard the sound of sirens and police whistles.

'Oh dear,' cried Mrs Giant. 'Whatever is that? I've never heard anything like it.'

26

Jackie and the Baked Bean Stalk

'Oh no,' groaned Jackie. 'It's the police, they must have come looking for me.'

Both the giants went white and then scrambled under the table, shaking with fear.

'This is all my fault,' thought Jackie miserably. 'Don't worry,' she called to the terrified giants, 'I'll sort this out.' And she grabbed two buckets of water and raced to the turret. Just as she got there, she heard a voice through a loud hailer.

'You in there, let Jackie out or we're coming in. Let her out first, then you come out with your hands up. No funny business, you're surrounded.'

At that moment, a bucket of cold water fell on the police sergeant. They all looked up and saw Jackie standing on the turret.

'Jackie!' yelled her father. 'Are you all right, love?'

'I'm fine, Dad, but I'm not coming down

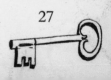

Would You Believe It?

until you stop being silly and threatening my friends, Mr and Mrs Giant. Tell all the policemen to go away.'

'Where are the giants?' shouted the police.

'They're under the kitchen table, trembling,' Jackie told them. 'You've scared them half to death and they're very nice, really they are.'

'They didn't try to eat you then?'

'Oh no,' Jackie told the amazed group. 'All their teeth have fallen out and they've retired.'

The policemen and the fire brigade and the doctors and the nurses all stared at Jackie with their mouths open in amazement.

'I'm going down now to tell Mr and Mrs Giant that it was all a mistake and in five minutes you can come in.'

Jackie went downstairs and told the

giants they could come out and no one
would harm them. Outside, the police
sergeant sent a message to Jackie's mum to
say that Jackie was safe. Soon, Mrs Giant
was giving them all tea in thimbles and
letting them taste her homemade baked
beans. When Jackie's dad said it was time
to go, they all walked to the top of
the beanstalk.

'I hope you won't go cutting it down this
time,' said the giant. 'We've enjoyed having
visitors again, haven't we Mother?'

'We most certainly have,' agreed Mrs
Giant. 'Particularly when they are well-
behaved girls, not at all like that nasty
Jack.'

The giant agreed to lower the
ambulance and the fire engine down with
a rope. Everyone said goodbye and began
to climb down the beanstalk. When they
got to the bottom, there was a whole army

of reporters and photographers and people
from the TV. Jackie was interviewed and
told them the whole story, which she
ended, 'and the giants are the nicest people
you ever met.'

The reporters were very keen to go up
the beanstalk and see for themselves but the
police sergeant blocked their way.

'No one is to go up there until this town
has decided what to do about this
beanstalk. I am going to leave a twenty-
four hour guard at the bottom and anyone
trying to go up the beanstalk will be
arrested.'

Just then, there came a shout from the
top of the beanstalk.

'One fire engine and one ambulance
coming down!'

They are scattered out of the way of the
fire engine and ambulance which landed
gently on all four wheels.

Jackie and the Baked Bean Stalk

Everyone cheered.

'Thank you very much,' yelled the police sergeant through the loud hailer.

'All right, now everyone can go home until we decide what is to be done with this, uh, baked bean stalk,' said the sergeant.

'We'll have a meeting in the town hall tonight!' cried the mayor. 'Everyone be there at seven o'clock.'

'Meeting? You must be mad,' cried someone. 'Two ugly great giants living above our town and you want to leave that beanstalk standing. Cut it down right now.'

'Yes,' chorused a group of people. 'Cut it down now. Or we'll be murdered in our beds.'

'Nonsense,' said the policeman, 'the giants are very nice.'

'He could have eaten me if he'd wanted to but he didn't,' cried Jackie indignantly.

Would You Believe It?

'Well we want that beanstalk down,' they grumbled.

All that day, Jackie tried to think of a way to help her new friends.

'It would be awful if the beanstalk were cut down and I could never see the giants again,' she thought and a tear ran down her cheek.

'I like the giants too, Jackie,' said her dad, giving her a hug. 'The trouble with people round here is they don't have enough to do. It was really bad news for this town when the steel mills closed.'

'I'm beginning to get an idea, Dad. The giants could bring work to this town.'

'How?'

'We could charge people if they wanted to come and see the beanstalk.'

'Yes,' cried her father. 'We could turn it into a giant Giant Theme Park.'

'All we have to do is convince the people

at the meeting tonight,' agreed Jackie.

That evening at seven o'clock, the whole town met in the town hall. All round were banners which read: NO GIANTS FOR TRUMPLINGTON. CUT THE STALK NOW! and there were shouts of 'Giants out, giants out, out, out.'

'Oh dear,' sighed Jackie.

'Don't you worry, love, just you wait till they've heard your idea.'

Then the mayor spoke.

'We are here to decide what to do about this baked bean stalk that has suddenly appeared in the middle of our town.'

'Cut it down!' shouted the crowd.

Jackie rushed up and grabbed the microphone.

'No, don't cut it down, please don't. My baked bean stalk could save this town.'

There was a murmur of confusion. 'Save the town! Destroy it more like.'

Would You Believe It?

'We've thought of a way that could put this town back to work,' yelled Jackie's dad.

The crowd looked at him in amazement.

'My Jackie thinks we should turn this town into a giant Giant Theme Park. Just think about it, already half the press of the world are here. Everyone will want to see the beanstalk. We could charge them to get near it. We could sell teas and make souvenirs, there would be a demand for hotels and restaurants and car parks. We could ask the giants if they would mind if visitors went up the beanstalk. Just think – work again and a future for our children.'

There was a shocked silence.

'Well!' said the mayor, 'what a novel idea, I'm all for it. Let's take a vote – who's for a giant Giant Theme Park in Trumplington?'

'Can you promise us the giants won't

turn nasty?'

'They're lovely, really they are,' Jackie told the crowd, 'and they just love having visitors.'

'So let's have a show of hands,' demanded the mayor. 'Those for?'

A sea of hands went up.

'Those against?'

There were only about twenty hands.

'The ayes have it!' yelled the mayor, jumping up and down with excitement. 'This is wonderful, now we've really got something to look forward to again.'

So the theme park was opened and soon the town was on every tourist map. Tens of thousands of people poured in to meet the giants, and so Trumplington became a happy and prosperous town again, thanks to Jackie and her giant friends.

Someone Elsie

—

PIPPA GOODHART

Rose and Daisy skipped on the pavement
outside Rose's house.

> *Skip and hop. Skip and hop.*
> *Keep on going. Never stop.*
> *Forwards, backwards, fast and slow.*
> *Jumping high and jumping low.*

Skipping was their craze at the moment.

'Bet you can't do this!' shouted Daisy.

Her skipping rope slapped the pavement

and her ponytail flap-flopped as she
jumped twice between each circling of
the rope.

'Bet I can! Bet I can even do it on just
one leg! Watch this!' Rose did two hops,
then tangled in the rope and fell. Daisy
laughed.

'Knew you couldn't do it!'

'I could if I didn't have to turn the rope
at the same time. My mum told me what
they used to do when she was at school.
They had two people holding an end of
the rope each and turning it so that
another person could jump in the middle.
You can do all kinds of different skipping
that way, even having your hands in your
pockets or something.'

'But we'd need three people for that,' said
Daisy. 'And there's only two of us.'

'Then let's go and find someone else to
join in.'

37

Would You Believe It?

'Where?'

'We could try the park.'

So Rose and Daisy rolled their ropes round and round the handles and stuffed them into their pockets. Rose shouted to her mum in the house, 'We're off to play in the park!' and her mum shouted back, 'Make sure and be back in time for tea!'

'We will!'

Side by side, with arms linked behind their backs, Rose and Daisy skipped their feet down the road to the park. And all the time they were looking for someone else to join their game.

'If we find somebody, you won't make her your best friend instead of me, will you?' asked Daisy.

'Of course not,' said Rose. 'Not so long as you don't make friends with her and then not want me for a friend any more.'

'We've got to find somebody that's not

38

too bossy.'

'Somebody who'll like our ideas.'

There were old people in the park and lots of dogs and boys playing football, but there didn't seem to be any girls. Rose and Daisy ran along the paths and around a corner and under an arch into a quiet part of the park and there they saw . . .

'There's somebody there!' said Daisy. But Rose laughed. 'That's only a girl made of stone! It's cold, and I think it's old. Look at her silly long dress!'

'Yes,' said Daisy. 'And look at her funny name!'

It had 'Elsie' carved into the stone block below the stone girl's feet.

Daisy did a big curtsey and put on a posh voice, 'So delighted to meet you, Elsie.'

But Elsie didn't move. She stood tall on top of the stone block and she didn't say a thing.

Would You Believe It?

'Stupid thing!' said Daisy, and she kicked at the hard stone, and that hurt her foot.

'Ow!'

Elsie looked down at Rose and Daisy with a steady stare that didn't blink.

'What are you staring at?' Rose asked stone Elsie. 'You hurt Daisy, you did! You're mean and . . . !' But Daisy put a hand on Rose's arm to shush her.

'Stop it, Rose! Look at that!'

A small stone tear, clear blue and glistening, slid slowly down Elsie's stone cheek. It tippled down onto her dress, down and down, then fell from the hem and landed – plink! – on the stone block below.

Daisy picked up the tear and held it to the light. 'It's beautiful,' she said. 'It's like a tiny perfect pear.'

'Give it to me,' said Rose. 'I want to see.'

'But it's mine,' said Daisy. 'I made her cry it. If you want one of your own, then you

make her do another.'

'It's mean to make her cry,' said Rose.

'No, it's not,' said Daisy. 'Elsie's only a stone girl. It's not the same.'

So Rose did make Elsie cry again. They both did. They said horrible things to Elsie, and watched the tears fall – plink, plink, plink – onto the stone below. The tears came pink and green and orange and mauve and gold. And the more colours Elsie wept, the greyer she became.

'She's going more grey,' said Daisy.

'That's because the sun's going down,' said Rose, but she didn't sound sure. She looked at Daisy, and Daisy looked at her. 'I think we've got enough tears now. We'd better get back for tea or Mum'll be cross.'

'Yes,' agreed Daisy. 'I'm bored of this game anyway.'

So Rose and Daisy filled their pockets with glinting, coloured, stone tears and left

Would You Believe It?

Elsie alone in the park.

Under the arch and around the corner, and along the path and through the gates and onto the pavement, the tears hung heavy in their pockets. Rose and Daisy didn't join hands or skip. They didn't feel in the mood. They walked home slowly and a little sad, not talking. Their hands in their pockets chinked the stone tears together and they made a lonely sound.

After tea, the evening darkened around Rose's house. Rose rolled the tears through her fingers. She felt the soft, round, blunt end at the bottom of each tear and she felt the sharp pointed top that pricked her fingers and hurt, and Rose wondered. She turned on her bedside light and looked at the tears, pale and see-through where they bulged; thick with dark colour at their point, and she thought.

Rose went to bed, but she couldn't sleep.

Someone Elsie

She heard her parents go to bed, and still
she couldn't sleep. The house settled to
stillness and all she could hear was the hum
of the fridge and the tick tock of the clock.
Then a sudden scatter of small stones at
her window made Rose gasp in fright.

'Who's there?' she asked the dark.

Rose sat up in bed, her heart thump-
thumping high in her throat. 'Who is it?'
she said again. She thought that it might
be Elsie – Elsie standing stiff and staring up
at the window and wanting to shout at
Rose the way that Rose had shouted at
her. Rose hugged her blanket tight around
herself. Then she tiptoed to her window,
where she peeked between the curtain and
the window edge and looked down to
the garden.

There was a girl there, but it wasn't Elsie.
It was Daisy, pale and hazy in the
moonlight. She was calling out something

43

that Rose couldn't hear. Rose pulled back the curtains and opened the window.

'Daisy, why are you here in the middle of the night?' she asked, although she thought she could guess.

'I couldn't sleep,' said Daisy. 'I've been lying in bed and thinking and I've been feeling the tears, and do you know what, Rose? They're warm. Do you suppose . . .?'

'That Elsie is real?' said Rose. 'She can't be, can she? But what if she is? Let's go and see.'

So Rose and Daisy, dressed in nighties, crept away from the warm hug of home and into the cold empty night that changed things. Their breath came out as steam and their bare feet were so cold that they felt as if they burned on the pavement. They ran. But they ran strangely, awkwardly, because all the way, their hands carefully cradled the stone tears

44

and didn't drop one.

Rose and Daisy ran back to Elsie, Elsie pale and grey in the moonlight. And Elsie wasn't asleep any more than they were. She still stared down at Rose and Daisy. Rose and Daisy hung their heads.

'We've come to give your tears back,' said Rose. 'We're sorry for what we did and what we said.'

Then Rose and Daisy held up their hands full of tears. Daisy asked, 'Elsie, please, will you be our friend?' And Elsie's sad stone face melted into movement and lived, there in the moonlight. She blinked slowly and her mouth curled gently into an almost smile. Then Elsie stepped stiffly, one foot, then two, down from her high stone block. She held out her hands and Rose and Daisy tipped them full of the heavy warm tears. With each tear she took, Elsie grew less grey and her hands grew warm.

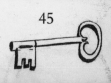

45

Would You Believe It?

And with each tear they gave, Rose and Daisy felt lighter and began to laugh. And Elsie smiled.

'Elsie, can you skip?' asked Daisy.

'Will you skip with us?' asked Rose. 'Please, Elsie?'

So they skipped together in the pale soft moonlight, all looking soft and grey and the same. If you had been watching them, you wouldn't have known which was Daisy or which was Elsie or which was Rose, which was the long dress and which were the nighties. Two turned the rope and one skip-danced in the middle, then they swapped around and did it again another way, taking turns.

> *Skip and hop, skip and hop.*
> *Trip the skip, trip, slip and stop.*
> *Rose and Daisy on the ground.*
> *Rose and Daisy look around.*

Someone Elsie

Rose and Daisy look up high.
Elsie, Elsie, don't you cry.
Elsie, Rose and Daisy, learn to fly!

And as the night reached morning, there they all were, stretching and yawning in the first slanting sunlight of the day. It lit three sleepy girls slumping together as they walked under the arch and round the corner and headed for home. The sun showed that each one of them was as bright and real as the other. Daisy blinked tired eyes and took hold of one of Elsie's hands and told her, 'Rose and I were looking for you. We needed someone else to play.'

'Yes,' said Rose as she took Elsie's other warm hand. 'And you really are Someone, Elsie, aren't you?'

'I am,' said Elsie.

Unlucky Charm

—

DOUGLAS HILL

When Grandad came in wearing a special smile, Ben knew what it meant. Grandad had been rummaging in junk shops again, and had found a treasure.

'This is supposed to be a lucky charm from Europe somewhere,' Grandad said, taking something from his pocket. 'Very old.'

It was a tiny figurine, no bigger than Grandad's thumb. Its skinny body, spidery

arms and legs, and little round head were carved from soft wood and painted a nasty yellowish-green, with a black line for a mouth and two dots for eyes. And it was wonderfully smooth and polished.

'It looks like an alien, or a goblin,' Ben said.

'It's ugly enough,' said Ben's mum, smiling.

'Was it expensive?' Ben's dad asked.

Grandad chuckled. 'No, the shopkeeper seemed glad to get rid of it. Anyway, it's for you, Ben. Young folk need good luck, more than old ones.'

'Thanks, Grandad,' Ben said happily, and took it off to his room.

Ben was a sturdy eleven-year-old, with dark hair and a cheerful face. And he was smiling extra-cheerfully as he looked around his room for a place to put the figurine.

49

Would You Believe It?

He always liked Grandad's surprise gifts.
But then he liked his Grandad a lot – not
just because of the gifts, but because
Grandad was so much *fun*. Ben's mum
often said that, although Grandad was old
and white-haired, on the inside he was still
about eleven. Which was probably why he
and Ben got on so well.

Ben reached up to set the figurine on a
shelf – but nearly dropped it when he felt a
sudden pain in his hand, as if he had been
jabbed by a pin or stung by an insect.

Putting the figurine down, he saw a dot
of blood on his thumb. But there wasn't
anything sharp on the figurine. It must've
been a bug, he thought . . .

'You wouldn't hurt me, would you?' he
said to the figurine, smiling. 'You're my
lucky charm.'

That night, the wail of a car alarm outside

50

brought Ben awake. But when it stopped, he heard another sound in the darkness of his room. A thin *hissing*, which made his skin crawl.

He switched on his bedside light, and the hissing stopped. But his skin crawled again, when he spotted a glint of yellow-green on the floor.

The little figurine was lying in the middle of the room. Not by the wall, as if it had simply fallen off the shelf, but halfway between the wall and Ben's bed.

And, for an instant, the thin line of the figurine's mouth had seemed to be *open*. Showing tiny, needle-sharp teeth.

Ben sat in a huddle, watching. But nothing happened. The figurine lay still and soundless, its mouth a painted line again.

This is silly, Ben told himself. That thing can't move, or hiss. It probably just fell and

bounced. And I *imagined* that its mouth was open. I *must* have . . .

He slid out of bed, grabbed an empty water glass and used it to scoop up the figurine. Then he put it back on the shelf, and placed the glass over it.

'That should hold you,' he muttered. But it took him a long time to get back to sleep. And he left the light on.

In the morning his mum, coming in to wake him, saw the figurine with the glass over it. 'Keeping it covered?' she laughed. 'It isn't *that* ugly.'

Ben managed a smile. The glass over the figurine did look a bit silly, and the thing itself seemed totally harmless in daylight.

But then he had a clear, chilling memory of what it had looked like when he had first turned on the light. And he left the glass where it was.

He wanted to tell Grandad, right away.

Unlucky Charm

But Grandad usually stayed in his room in the morning, while everyone was rushing to work or school. And Ben knew better than to tell his mum and dad. They'd just laugh, and say he'd been dreaming.

But after school, before his parents got home, Ben told Grandad the whole story. And Grandad didn't laugh, but listened carefully.

'How strange,' Grandad said. 'Could be that's why the man in the shop was glad to be rid of the thing. Let's go look at it.'

On Ben's shelf, the figurine was still inside its glass prison. But Ben saw that the glass had *moved*.

'Grandad!' he gasped. 'I didn't put it that close to the edge of the shelf!'

Grandad frowned. 'Are you sure?'

'Really!' Ben insisted. 'Maybe the thing was *moving* the glass, from the inside! So it would fall off the edge, and be free!'

Would You Believe It?

'Could be,' Grandad said slowly. 'If it really can come alive . . .'

He took up the glass, with the figurine held in it. And, for an instant, Ben thought he saw the figurine's eyes flare a dark, hate-filled red.

'I'll keep it in my room,' Grandad decided. 'Safe in a draw. And I'll do some reading – see if there's anything about things like this.'

Ben nodded nervously. Grandad had a great many old books about magic and witchcraft. Maybe they could help . . .

That night, even though Grandad had taken charge of the figurine, Ben kept his bedside light on. And he was glad of it, in the middle of the night, when a wild horror-dream jolted him awake and the light showed him a *real* horror.

The figurine was on his bed. Creeping

towards him, hissing, its needle-fangs
glinting, its eyes flaring red . . .

Ben felt as if he were encased in ice,
barely able to breathe. Yet as he stared at
the little horror, it went still, becoming a
lifeless figurine again.

Then Ben jumped as his door crashed
open. Grandad rushed in, his white hair
rumpled, with a faded robe over baggy
pyjamas.

'*There* it is,' he said, scowling. 'It woke me
up when it got the drawer open, but I
didn't see where it went.'

'It . . . it *is* alive . . .' Ben breathed,
shivering.

'Seems so,' Grandad agreed. 'But I read
something about things like this. I think it
can only come alive when nobody's
actually *looking* at it.'

'What *is* it?' Ben whispered.

'A bit of nasty magic,' Grandad said. 'I

found something in a book about evil
wizards making such things to give to their
enemies.' He sighed. 'Not a lucky charm
after all. Sorry, Ben.'

'That's all right, Grandad, you didn't
know,' Ben said. 'What'll we do with it?'

Grandad gathered up the figurine. 'I'll
stay up and watch it tonight,' he said.
'Tomorrow I'll find a way to destroy it.'

After a disturbed night, Ben was only half-
awake all next day, which annoyed his
teachers. But he came fully alert when he
got home, and went to Grandad's room.

On the table, he saw the figurine –
under the glass, with a heavy book on top
– looking as smooth and shiny as ever,
completely unharmed.

'I tried lots of things,' Grandad said
glumly. 'I tried to burn it, I tried to cut it
up with a knife, I tried to smash it with a

56

hammer, I put it in boiling water . . .
Nothing. That shiny paint is probably a
magical protection.'

Ben stared at the figurine's yellow-green
smoothness. 'What can we do then? Chuck
it in the river?'

Grandad shook his head. "That would
just set it free. No, we'll keep trying. There'll
be *some* way to get rid of it.'

That evening, pretending that Grandad
was helping Ben with a school project, the
two of them set to work. They soaked the
figurine in vinegar, in bleach, in boiling oil
– they attacked it with a hacksaw and an
axe – they baked it in the oven and froze it
in the freezer . . .

And none of that had any effect at all.

So, telling Ben to stay clear, Grandad
tried more dangerous ways – pouring acid
on the figurine, using a power drill on it,
jamming its head into an electric socket.

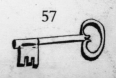

Would You Believe It?

But none of that worked either. And by Ben's bedtime, they had run out of ideas.

'I'll do some more reading,' Grandad said. 'And I'll keep watch on it tonight. I don't need much sleep.'

Ben did, after two troubled nights. But even so, worrying about the figurine made him sleep restlessly. And, again, another nightmare dragged him awake in the middle of the night.

Gazing fearfully around his room, he expected to see the figurine coming at him, fangs glittering. But there was no sign of it.

Yet he still felt shivery and uneasy, with a sort of vague dread. So he decided that talking to Grandad might make him feel better.

Quietly, he went along to Grandad's room. Grandad had planned to sit up all night watching the figurine, so it couldn't come alive. But he was slumped in his

armchair, sound asleep, snoring softly.

Ben went cold with fright. If Grandad was sleeping, not looking at the figurine, it would have come alive. So *where was it*?

Then, horrified, Ben saw the yellow-green shape.

It was clinging to Grandad's wrist, its tiny fanged mouth fastened to one of the wrist's big blue veins.

'No!' Ben choked, and leaped forward. The figurine raised its head, its mouth smeared with blood. But because it was being looked at, it went still, and Ben furiously knocked it away from Grandad's wrist.

'Umph . . .' Grandad grunted, coming awake. 'What's . . . *ouch*!' And he peered at the small trail of blood on his wrist.

'It was *biting* you, Grandad!' Ben said.

Grandad scowled, rubbing his wrist. 'A bloodsucker, eh? Thanks, Ben – I'd have

59

been in a bad way if you hadn't come in. Where is it?'

Ben looked around – but there was no sign of the figurine. 'It's gone!'

'We'd better find it,' Grandad said grimly. 'Before it bites someone else.'

Finding a three-inch object – one that could move and hide, when it wasn't being looked at – began to seem impossible. It took a long time just to search Grandad's cluttered room. Then there was the rest of the house, where they had to be careful not to wake Ben's parents, though Ben did peek silently into their bedroom, to make sure his mum and dad weren't being attacked.

By the time the sun was rising, they still had the kitchen to search, not to mention the attic. And they were bleakly aware that the little horror might have crept around *behind* them, to hide someplace they had

already searched.

They paused for a rest in the kitchen, where Grandad made a pot of tea while Ben drooped at the table. They were still wearily sitting there when Ben's mum wandered in, yawning.

'Goodness!' she said, startled. 'Early birds!' She peered at them. 'You two look like you've hardly slept. What's wrong?'

'Nothing,' Grandad said quickly. 'Ben had a bad dream, and I was a bit wakeful, so we came out here.'

'Just as well it's Saturday,' Ben's mum said, picking up the teapot and pouring herself a cup.

'That'll be cold now,' Grandad said.

Mum nodded. 'I'll just warm it up, and make a fresh pot later.'

She opened the microwave, putting the cup in without looking while she set the timer, then closed the door. In less than a

minute, the microwave pinged.

Mum, busy with cereal boxes, glanced at Grandad. 'Get that for me, would you?'

Grandad opened the microwave door. Then he and Ben went very still, gaping with astonishment.

The inside of the microwave was covered with spots and smears of what looked like sticky dust. Yellow–green dust.

Ben and Grandad backed away, easing themselves out of the kitchen before Mum noticed anything. 'Now we know where it hid,' Ben murmured.

Grandad nodded. 'And the microwave heats things up from the *inside*, so the thing's magic covering didn't protect it. It must've got so hot it burst!'

They heard Mum's shriek from the kitchen, as she saw the mess.

'Let's hope she thinks something spilled earlier,' Grandad said, a little nervously,

Unlucky Charm

'and she didn't notice.'

Ben sighed. 'Anyway, I'm glad it's gone.'

'Me too,' Grandad agreed. 'But it's good to know that modern science can defeat evil magic.' He grinned. 'In case there's something funny about the *next* treasure I find.'

Cross Your Heart

—

GEOFF FOX

'Cross your heart and hope to die.'

The other girls at school said that all the time. I always hoped it would be a secret worth keeping, but usually it was just something sneaky about one of my friends – the sort of thing I wished they hadn't told me.

But this was different. For a start, we weren't in the school playground and it was a grown-up talking. What made it

Cross Your Heart

even more strange was that I didn't really know him. I'd said hello when I'd seen him working around the Manor House gardens that week. Now he was clipping one of the great yew bushes which lined the path where I was weeding the crazy-paving. Mum and I live in one of the cottages round the back of the Big House, as everyone calls it, and Mr Marsterson, who owns the Big House, said he'd give me two pounds an hour if I made a good job of the weeding. Since Mum couldn't spare much for pocket money, I said I'd do it, though it was a pretty boring way to spend the first Wednesday of the summer holidays, I can tell you.

'Cross your heart and hope to die if you ever tell anyone else what I'm going to tell you now.'

Now you may think I should have run for it back to our house but – honestly

Would You Believe It?

– would you? I mean, if anything
happened, I could still run for it, and I
could even see Mum only thirty metres
away, putting washing out in our garden.
Anyway, he was smiling as he said it –
with his eyes as well as his mouth, if you
know what I mean. It was a real smile. He
was maybe about the same age as my
grandpa. He must have worked outdoors a
lot; his face was very brown and had loads
of lines on it. His clothes seemed old-
fashioned somehow. In fact, he could have
been one of the farm labourers in the old
photographs Mum had shown me hanging
on the walls of Mr Marsterson's library. His
shirt was very faded and it had no collar.
His trousers were sort of furry – when we'd
been looking at the photographs, my mum
said that they used to make these really
hardwearing trousers out of moleskin in the
old days. He was wearing hob-nailed boots

Cross Your Heart

which looked as though he'd worn them
every day for years and years. His voice
was odd too – he had an accent I hadn't
heard before. He didn't come from our part
of the world, that's for sure.

He put his shears down beside him on a
garden bench and took a packet of
sandwiches and a vacuum flask out of an
old leather bag. I stopped weeding when he
spoke to me, and sat on a bench on the
other side of the path.

'You want to hear the story, don't you? I
can see you do. Well then, cross your heart
and hope to die, and then I'll tell it to you.'

He didn't say it like the girls at school
– I knew he really meant it.

'OK,' I said. I looked round to see if
Mum was watching, but she'd gone inside
for another load of washing or maybe a
cup of tea. Still, I turned my back to our
cottage when I crossed my heart in case

67

she was looking out of the window. I felt a bit of an idiot doing it, but I didn't feel scared. Not then. I really love stories and they're best when they're a bit shivery.

'Now *say* it as well. Say this: "I hope to die if ever I tell anyone the story you are going to tell me now".'

So I did.

'Well done.'

Then, instead of starting off, he suddenly went quiet. He was staring down the garden towards the old gatehouse which is one of my favourite bits of the Big House. It's hundreds of years old and it's got two small towers connected by an archway spanning a huge weatherbeaten oak door. The towers were really one-room cells, where they used to keep prisoners overnight when they were being taken for trial at the County Courts in the city. One cell had a little fireplace and that one was

for women. The men had to put up with
the cold and damp in the other cell.
Outside the gatehouse were a couple of
steps down to Manor Hill Lane which
drops down to the stone bridge over the
river. The first step is just an ordinary stone
step, but the second one is almost a metre
high. I have to take a bit of a run and a
jump to get up it, though someone has put
a couple of breezeblocks at one side for
people who don't like jumping. The
gatehouse was the only way you could
reach the Big House, since there were high
stone walls all around the garden. At least,
it used to be the only way.

The gardener was staring right through
the gatehouse, down the hill to Breedy
Water, which is what we all call the river
at this point. As I looked at him, I just
knew he was more frightened of telling this
story than I was of hearing it, even with all

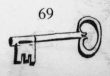

Would You Believe It?

that crossing-your-heart business. I know
that probably sounds crazy, but I knew it
was true. After a while, he seemed to
remember I was there, ready and listening.

'It was like this,' he began, as though he
didn't really want to get to the point. 'I'd
never worked in this part of the world until
this week, but I liked this place as soon as I
got here. Yesterday, I was going to weed the
crazy-paving – the job you've been doing
this morning. I'd just started work when Mr
Marsterson came out. Seems they were
going to make a hole in the old garden
wall because Mr Marsterson wanted to be
able to bring his car closer to the house
– he was fed up with leaving it outside
the gatehouse and his wife was always
going on about visitors not being able to
manage the step. So he asked me to go and
help the men he'd hired to knock a hole
through the wall.

Cross Your Heart

'It took us all day to make that hole. Not surprising, really, when you think the wall had been standing there for hundreds of years. Seemed a bit of a pity to me.'

I wasn't very interested in his story so far. I mean, what's worth crossing your heart and hoping to die about making a hole in a wall? But I said nothing. You wouldn't, would you?

'Then this morning, Mr Marsterson said I had to go and work on that flowerbed, just down there by the hole we'd made. He wanted the plants taking out and moving before he put the new drive in for this car. It was really misty early on today, before the sun began to burn it off. You'd still have been in bed, I shouldn't wonder. I was just bending down to dig out a clump of Michaelmas daisies, when I heard something, quite close by. A tap, tap, tapping sound. I thought it might have

71

Would You Believe It?

been a nuthatch or a woodpecker – or maybe a thrush cracking a shell on the path to get the snail out. Then there was another sound – sharper and louder – too. And I knew what that was, for certain. It was a horse's hoof, scraping on the stones we'd left lying around when we'd knocked the hole through the wall. So, of course, I looked up.'

The gardener stopped there, just when he'd got me really interested. I could feel the gooseflesh come up on my arms. It wasn't so much what he'd said – it was the way he was staring down towards the hole in the wall.

'Go on,' I said. 'Please. What happened next?' Though, you know, by this time I think I'd almost guessed. Anyone in our class at school would have known.

'It *was* a horse. A great black stallion – bigger than Mr Marsterson's hunter. And

on it, there was a rider. Tall, thin, in a long, long grey coat. Not like you see riders wearing round here. More like a highwayman's coat, if you know what I mean. And he had long leather riding boots with silver buckles on them. But the worst thing, you see, was his head. It was *loose*, like. Sort of lolling from side to side, almost falling onto his shoulders. And he had a tall hat with a feather – it looked as though it would topple off that head of his any minute, but it didn't. You should have seen his eyes. They were like two red fires deep inside black caves. Right up close to my face, he was tap, tap, tapping his leather boots with a riding crop. It had a silver handle shaped like a dog's head – I've never seen one like it.

'And there was another thing. He was dripping wet all over.'

The gardener was silent for a minute or

two, and so was I.

'Then the rider leant down towards me
and he said, very slowly like, "I've come
home at last, my friend. It's taken a while,
but we've made it. Eh, Vulcan? Lewis and
Vulcan, we've made it together, haven't
we?"

'And he smiled and patted his horse's
neck. He just sat there, staring down at me
with a thin smile on his face. Horse and
rider – they didn't move an inch for ages,
except for the man's head, rolling and
rocking from side to side. And the water,
dripping from his hat and that long coat. I
didn't dare say anything. Then he said,
"And you're the only one that knows I'm
back. Oh yes, Lewis is back. And he's never
going away again, my friend, no matter
what they try. Very good of them to make
an entrance in the old wall to let us in, eh,
Vulcan? And you, *you'll* tell no one we're

here. If you do . . ."

'Then he raised his riding crop and just flicked my shoulder with it – right here.'

The gardener leaned forward towards me across the path and pulled back his faded shirt. I could see a dark, sticky red weal across his left shoulder. It was oozing more than bleeding, if you know what I mean.

'Then the horseman spoke again. "So, you'll tell no one, else they'll come with their priests and their paraphernalia to trouble my peace. And I've earned my peace. I've waited a long time to come home. It's been a slow hard climb for the two of us, hasn't it, Vulcan? Now, cross your heart and hope to die if you tell anyone what you've seen this morning." So I did what he told me. And that's all he said. Mr Marsterson called me from the front door of the Big House just then, and when I

looked back for the horseman again, he'd gone. No sight nor sound of him. Except the paving stones were still glistening wet where they'd been standing.'

The gardener didn't say anything else, and neither did I. You see, I knew who the horseman was. His name was Lewis Dargent and long ago he was the owner of the Big House. Two-hundred-and-fifty-six years ago, as a matter-of-fact. Everyone who lived in our village knew the story of Lewis Dargent. Our teacher had told us about him just last Hallowe'en – that was how I knew the exact number of years. He was what my mum calls 'a bit of a Jack the Lad'. He drank too much red wine and he lost too much of his family's fortune gambling at cards. He let the farms around the Big House run down and he treated his servants and the farm labourers worse than his animals.

Cross Your Heart

There was one woman they called Old Ellen who had worked as a maid for Lewis's mother all her life. That didn't stop Lewis throwing her and her belongings out of her cottage onto the muddy lane when she was too feeble to work any more. Old Ellen didn't last long – she caught a fever at the parish workhouse. Before she died, the story goes, she sat bolt upright in bed and she screamed out a curse on her master.

'You'll die by Breedy Water, Lewis Dargent. And you'll find no rest in Heaven, and you'll find no rest in the fires of Hell. This is your fate, Lewis Dargent. You'll sweat and you'll strain and you'll climb up Manor Hill Lane back to the Big House by one cockerel-stride every month of every year.'

Then she lay back in her bed and, just once, she laughed long and loud. And that

was the last sound she ever made.

When he heard the story of Old Ellen's curse, Lewis laughed too and called her a crazy old crone, and so did most of the villagers. The river was only two or three feet deep, they said, and no one had ever drowned in it. And as for all the nonsense about cockerel-strides – if anyone ever climbed up Manor Hill just a few inches every month, they'd all be dead and buried long before he got there, so why should they worry? But it was such a strange curse that people couldn't quite forget it. Some of them told the story to their children, and then they passed it on to their children. So that was how my teacher got to hear of it.

And, you know, a couple of years later, Lewis *did* die by Breedy Water. One stormy night he rode out to a neighbour's house to play cards and to drink a glass or two of red wine. He lost a lot of money and drank

more than a glass or two. So he was in a foul mood when he whipped his horse Vulcan through the rain and mud, down to the stone bridge over Breedy Water. Vulcan had a temper to match his master's and maybe he didn't much like being kept out of his stable on a night like that, and maybe he didn't like being whipped for no fault of his own. Whatever the reason, when they were crossing the bridge, Vulcan reared up and tipped his master head-over-heels into the river.

With all the rain there had been, Breedy Water was a swirling muddy brown torrent that night – too much for a strong swimmer, never mind a drunk. Vulcan made his own way home up the hill, and when the servants discovered him wandering about in the stable yard, they raised the alarm. They found Lewis just after dawn, caught among some willows almost a mile

downstream. Some said he hadn't drowned
because his neck was broken first from the
fall. But one way or another, he was as
dead as a stone.

That was when people in the village
remembered Old Ellen's curse. Sure enough,
he'd drowned in Breedy Water, but what
about those cockerel-strides? Some of the
villagers were so frightened they went and
found a cockerel and measured how far he
walked with one stride. I asked my teacher
how they could have done that, but she
didn't know. Then they paced out the
distance from the bridge up Manor Hill
Lane to the walls of the garden and – you
don't have to believe this if you don't want
to – they reckoned it would take Lewis
two-hundred-and-fifty-six years to reach
the Big House at one cockerel-stride every
month. Honestly, that's the exact figure
they came up with, as sure as I'm telling

you this story. So you can guess that everyone in our class had a good time making spooky wailing sounds and screaming pretend screams when our teacher told us the tale.

Lewis's nephew, when he inherited the Manor House, decided something had to be done to keep the ghost from ever getting into the gardens. He thought the old walls would keep Lewis out, but he wasn't so sure about the gatehouse. So he said to his steward, 'We'll keep him out. I want you to build a huge step up to the gatehouse so that no cockerel-strider, living or dead, will ever get up. He'll not even reach the gatehouse, never mind get through into the garden.'

And that's why the step up the gatehouse is so high. Or that's what our teacher said.

'It was Lewis Dargent's ghost you saw!' I said to the gardener. Except the gardener

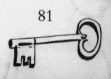

81

Would You Believe It?

had disappeared. How he did that without
making any noise on the stone path with
those hobnailed boots on, I don't know. I
never saw him go. One minute he was
there, the next he was gone. No one at the
Big House or in the village ever saw him
again. He didn't collect any wages from Mr
Marsterson. He left his sandwiches and his
flask on the bench – I've still got the flask
in my bedroom, so I know I didn't dream it
all. And no one has ever seen a rider in a
long grey coat, dripping wet all over, on
a black stallion, in the gardens of the
Manor House.

I've never told anyone what the
gardener told me, not even my mum.
Somehow, I wanted to keep it a secret until
I found the right person to tell it to. No,
I've never told *anyone*. Not till now, that is.

Cross your heart and hope to die, if you
ever tell . . .

Jack and the
Dream Maker

—

ELINOR HODGSON

In a forest not far from here lives a Dream
Maker with wild hair and a multicoloured
cloak. By day he makes daydreams and by
night he makes sweet dreams. The recipes
are secret and only the Dream Maker will
ever know them.

Once the dreams are ready, he boils
them, turning them into steam dreams
which rise up into the air. They travel for
miles, like invisible balloons, caught up in

Would You Believe It?

air currents and blown by the wind to the far corners of the earth.

Many dreams settle on clouds and every so often too many collect in one. All together they are so heavy that the cloud can't hold them anymore, so it bursts and the dreams plummet back to earth in raindrops.

Some fall on the ground and sink into the earth where the worms drink them. Some fall into the sea where the fish swallow them. Some fall on us. When dreamdrops land on humans and other animals, the dream slips out of the rain and through the skin. It flows round your bloodstream until it reaches your brain and settles in your subconscious until the right time comes for you to dream it.

Jack was a big dreamer. In his dreams he could do anything. At night he won battles against the Underbed Monsters, armed

Jack and the Dream Maker

with a shield and a lightning bolt.
Sometimes his school turned into a
haunted dungeon and he braved ghosts and
dragons to lead his classmates to freedom.
By day, when his lessons were dull, he rode
dinosaurs across the desert or explored the
jungle, swinging from tree to tree like a
monkey and wrestling with giant snakes.
Other times, he became the hero of his
favourite computer game with superpowers
and an endless number of lives, a match
for anyone.

But one day, his dreams became
nightmares. At night the Underbed
Monsters came for him before he was
ready. They turned his lightning bolt into a
plastic spoon and his shield into a paper
plate. They gnashed their bloody teeth and
grasped at him while he ran without
moving until, terrified, he woke himself up.

After that, they came for him every

night. Each time he woke himself up, but even awake he was sure he could hear them rumbling in the dark under his bed, and each night they got closer.

His daydreams stopped too. All he could think about now was how scared he was of sleep.

Each night he piled his clothes up around his bed to seal the gaps and stop the Underbed Monsters from getting him. But they still came. He tried leaving the light on while he slept. But they still came.

Once he was awake he would lie in the dark for hours with his head under the covers, even though he got too hot. He was frightened to turn the light on in case an Underbed Monster ripped off his arm in the gap between his bed and the table.

One night he was still awake when his mum came in to turn off the light. 'Please don't turn it off,' begged Jack.

Jack and the Dream Maker

'Why, Jack?' asked his mum. 'You can't
sleep with the light on.'

'I can't sleep at all!' he cried. 'Every
night I have the same nightmare and it gets
worse each time. I'm scared tonight that if
I sleep, I'll never wake up again.'

'You spend too much time on the
computer,' said Jack's mother, 'just be brave.'

'I can't,' Jack sighed.

'Of course you can,' said his mother,
more softly this time, 'but having the light
on won't help. You must go and find the
Dream Maker and tell him what's
happened. I'm sure he doesn't realise his
dreams are turning into nightmares. He
only makes sweet dreams so, unless
someone tells him, he won't know to do
anything about it. People all over the
worlds could be having bad dreams and if
you want to be a hero, this is the best
chance you've ever had!'

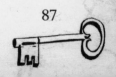

Would You Believe It?

Jack wasn't so sure – he'd never heard of the Dream Maker. It was probably a story she was making up on the spot to try and distract him. 'How will I find him?' Jack asked. 'I don't know where he lives or even if he exists!'

'It's easy,' said Jack's mum, ignoring his last comment. 'He puts a doorway to his home in every dream. If you really want to find it, you will, and it will take you to him. But you can only go there in your dreams, so you'd better get to sleep quickly!'

Maybe it *was* true, Jack thought. Now he wanted to get to sleep so much he couldn't. He tried to sleep diagonally. He tried to curl himself up into a tiny ball. He tried putting his pillows at the other end of the bed. Nothing worked. Until, just when he thought he would never sleep again, he did.

Once again the Underbed Monsters

came to get him, but this time Jack didn't wake up and he moved when he ran, out of his room, down the stairs, out of the house, and down the street. He didn't dare look behind him; he knew the monsters were following from their eerie howls. He ran and ran until he came to the end of his street and saw a house he had never seen before. It was inside out. As he looked through each window to see if anyone was inside, he found himself looking outside.

One window looked out on to the beach of a tropical island. Through another, he saw an oasis in a desert. Through the third, he saw the moon as if it were just a step away. But there was no door . . .

Just as the monsters appeared, so did a doorway and Jack fell inside. Standing with his back to him was a tiny man, no bigger than Jack himself, with frizzy hair and a multicoloured coat, stirring a sizzling pot

89

and singing to himself.

'Excuse me,' said Jack, panting for breath, 'I'm sorry to disturb you but I'm looking for the Dream Maker.'

The little man turned round, revealing the brightest green eyes and bushiest eyebrows Jack had ever seen.

'Look no further,' said the Dream Maker, smiling. 'You've found him. But who are you?'

'I'm Jack,' said Jack. 'I've come to tell you that your dreams have gone bad.'

The Dream Maker's smile disappeared. He went scarlet. Steam poured from his ears and he pressed his face so close to Jack's that his eyes crossed.

'Whaaaaaaaaat?' he roared. The whole house shook. 'Whaaaaaaaaat did you say?'

Jack thought of the monsters waiting for him outside ready to tear his flesh from his bones and stayed, trembling, where he was.

Jack and the Dream Maker

'P-p-please don't be angry,' he stammered. 'I know that you don't make bad dreams deliberately. I used to have wonderful dreams day and night but I don't anymore. I just wanted to tell you because I'd like to have them back.'

The Dream Maker raised a hairy eyebrow and looked hard at Jack. Then he stepped back, rubbed his head and thought for a while. 'Go down to my library,' he said, 'and get me every dream recipe book you can find.'

Jack did as he was told, but the library was round and every time he looked around, a shelf of new books appeared. It took forever, but eventually he staggered back to the Dream Maker with a huge pile. 'You must go now, Jack,' said the Dream Maker, 'it's time for you to get up.'

Before Jack could ask what would happen next, the Dream Maker had

Would You Believe It?

disappeared and Jack was in his bed with his mum gently waking him up.

'How did you sleep?' asked Jack's mother.

'Fine, thank you,' said Jack, and slipped past her into the bathroom before she could ask any more questions.

At school that day, Jack daydreamed about the Dream Maker. In his inside-out house, the Dream Maker was reading through his recipe books to see if he could find the source of the nightmares. He found nothing; the recipes were for sweet dreams. He would have to follow the dreams and see what happened to them on their journey. Maybe someone was poisoning them.

The Dream Maker boiled a fresh mixture of happy endings and as the last molecule steamed up the chimney he took off after them. They travelled halfway

Jack and the Dream Maker

round the world, over Europe and America,
to Australia, where they settled in a cloud.
The Dream Maker followed fast behind.
He too sat on the cloud and made it so
heavy that it burst and the dreams fell out
in raindrops. He'd never seen it happen
before and watched entranced as one
landed on a young girl sleeping peacefully
under the stars. He stayed to watch her
dream. Within minutes, her face had
contorted with fear and she woke up
shivering and afraid. Jack had been telling
the truth but the cause remained a
mystery. Suddenly fearful himself, the
Dream Maker went home to think again.

When he arrived, the answer was
waiting for him. As he walked into his
hallway, a dark stranger approached him
– a little man about his height with the
same bright green eyes but dressed from
top to toe in grey and black, like the dark

half of himself. They walked towards each other, eyes sparking fire. 'How dare you enter my house?' they shouted.

Blind with rage, the Dream Maker stormed up to his dark twin and prodded him in the chest. It was hard and cold as glass.

The Dream Maker was looking at his own reflection. He was covered in grime from top to toe. He stamped his feet and a cloud of dust jumped from his boots. A filthy fingerprint sat on the mirror. The only clean things were his teeth when he laughed out loud at his mistake.

It took him the rest of the day to get clean. But he had the answer; if the dirt in the air could do that to him, imagine what it did to the dream mixture. 'Filthy humans,' he snorted. 'Think they're so advanced, but look what they've done with their knowledge and their chemicals – they

deserve nightmares!'

But he thought about Jack and the girl he had watched in Australia. He had to do something, but even with the world's biggest vacuum cleaner he couldn't clear air so foul.

He went back to his books. Once again he found nothing until, just before nightfall, he read a recipe for dreams destined to travel through the earth's atmosphere. A silvery metal alloy, tough enough to take the hottest and coldest temperatures and the most vicious gases in our universe. Mixed with the dreams, at the steam stage, it would form a protective coating around them; sealing their contents safe from harm and evaporating at their final destination. He had just enough time before Jack slept to create it.

Deep in the vaults of his house is a room, shaped like the periodic table, with

95

separate chambers for each element. Each chamber travels down into the roots of the earth and as long as the Dream Maker treats the contents with respect, they will be filled to the brim with each element in its purest form, forever.

The Dream Maker collected his ingredients and, as he boiled fresh dreams, added them carefully to the mixture. With a new silver sheen, the steam dreams shimmered towards the sky. But the Dream Maker had one special delivery before he could rest. He caught the last dream in a tiny phial and sped it straight to the eyelids of sleeping Jack.

That night, Jack conquered the Underbed Monsters once more. And if you look, carefully, at the clouds when the sun is behind them, you will see that some of them have silver linings.

A Family Like Mine

Question:

What do you get when you cross a spitfire
and a ballet dancer with a Christmas runaway,
a familiar face from the past, two terrapins,
four goldfish and a woman who makes
strange goat noises?

Answer:

You get a brilliant collection of stories about
the remarkable ups and downs of family life.

What's Cool About School

Question:

What do you get when you cross
a multi-coloured woollen worm,
a comical pencil and a hairless bear
with Aladdin's basket, a space-craft tree
and the world's biggest cucumber?

Answer:

You get a brilliant collection of stories
about the fun and the frights of school.

Give Me Some Space!

Question:

What do you get when you cross a disobedient broomstick and a special silver pig with a miraculous sunflower, a billion stars, a big black hole and a toaster that talks?

Answer:

You get a brilliant collection of stories about the marvels of space and science.